Second Chance Love

Whiskey Run: Sugar

Hope Ford

Second Chance Love © 2022 by Hope Ford

Editor: Kasi Alexander

Cover Design: Cormar Covers

Cover Models: Kevin Davis and Emilie Beining

Image Photographer: CJC Photography

All rights reserved.

No part of this book may be reproduced in any form or by any electronic or mechanical means, including information storage and retrieval systems, without written permission from the author, except for the use of brief quotations in a book review.

Chapter 1

Nash

I pull through the gated entrance and wave at the security guard as I drive by. Looking at the nondescript building in front of me there's no indication of the goings-on inside. You can't look at a building and know about the blood, sweat, and tears that are poured into it, and that's exactly what Walker, I, and the rest of the team have done with our business. This building, on the edge of Whiskey Run, houses the elite Ghost Team. We are all ex-military mercenaries that help people. We travel all over the world, wherever we're called and save those that need it and then are out before any credit is given.

Thinking of all of the missions that I've been on the last several years, some of them stick out more than others, but every one of them was important. Every one of them made a difference. Knowing that makes what I'm about to do even harder.

I get out of the car and walk slowly into the building already dreading the conversation that I know is coming. I stop at the front desk and Brook, Walker's wife and assistant, looks at me in surprise. Usually, I'm in a rush and wave a hello as I go by. So when I stop, she glances up to me. "Hey, Nash! You okay?"

I nod my head and point toward Walker's door. I let out a big breath. "Yeah... I'm okay. Is he in?"

She nods. "Yep. He's in his office."

"Great," I murmur to her as I walk past and then knock on Walker's door. I hear him say, "Come in" and I take a deep breath while pulling back my shoulders before pushing open the door.

"Hey man, what's up?" he says when he sees me. Walker is more like a brother to me. He is the one that financially set this whole thing up and brought me on. In the beginning, I went on every and any mission that I could. Even when I wasn't necessarily needed, I still went.

It's like it was in my blood, the need to save people and make a difference. I had to prove myself. When I married Emery, I should have settled down and stayed home more, but I didn't. And even though she told me over and over that she wasn't happy, I never fully grasped that, and it wasn't until she served me with the divorce papers that it hit me and I knew I had fucked up. For almost a year now, we've been apart. It's been the worst year of my life. I know I have to change things, and it all starts right here in this moment.

My lack of response has Walker looking at me with his arms over his chest. "What's going on, Nash?"

I take a deep breath. It's now or never. I just hope it's not too late. "It's time."

Walker's eyes widen as he stares back at me. He knows exactly what I'm saying to him. It's only two words, but he knows. I've told him over and over that I'm going to get Emery back. And he knows what I'm going to have to do to do it.

Walker repeats what I said. "It's time?" But he asks it as a question instead of a statement.

I nod. "Yes. I'm going to need to step back. No more missions for me." The truth is in this past year, I've cut back a whole lot. I've only gone when it was absolutely necessary and there were lives on the line if I didn't.

But now we are at a point where we are fully

staffed. We can promote some of the guys to take over some more, and I can put 100 percent effort in getting Emery back. It's exactly what I should have done before the divorce went through.

I expect an argument from Walker, but he surprises me. "Okay. So what do we need to do? What do we need to put in place?"

I rear back in surprise. "You're okay with this?"

Walker leans over, putting his hands on his desk, and looks at me. "Maybe last year, I wouldn't have understood, but now that I have Brook, I completely get it, and we're going to make this work. You are still a partner in this company and always will be. You've put in your time, Nash. Hell, you've put in the time of three men. It's time you get what you deserve."

I put my hands in my front pockets and stare back at him. For the longest time, I didn't think I deserved anything. I was raised by shitty parents, and I turned to the Army when I was 18. I truly believe if I hadn't have done that, I would probably be dead right now under a bridge somewhere. The Army taught me a lot about being a man. And I can't believe that Emery fell in love with me. I did everything wrong, and she probably hates me now, but I can't give up.

I need to right all of my wrongs, and I need to win her back. It almost seems impossible going by the way she never wants to talk to me when I go and see her. I shake my head and try to get the thoughts out of my head. I can't start thinking negatively. That's not going to help at all. I clear my throat and look at Walker. "I'm thinking that we should promote Colt. I think he can handle it."

Walker nods his head. "I agree. I was sort of thinking the same thing. Why don't we get a meeting together sometime later today and go over the changes that are going to be taking place?"

I nod at him. "That sounds like a good idea."

I turn on my heel to walk out, but Walker stops me before I get through the door. "Hey man, are you okay with all of this?"

I sort of wince as I look back at him. Walker knows me better than most. He knows me as an adrenaline junkie, and there's no doubt he's wondering if I'm going to be able to do this or not. Can I really step away? But I don't know how to explain it except be honest with him. "I'm going to miss the missions, but there's no way it can compare to how much I miss her. I have to get her back, Walker."

He looks at me worriedly. "I got your back, man. Anything you need." I nod and go out the door with my head down as I walk toward my office. I think that taking a backseat role with the Ghost Team is going to be the easy part. Winning back Emery is a completely different story.

Chapter 2

Emery

"So have you always lived in Whiskey Run?"

I'm doing my best to appear interested, but not too interested in the man sitting across from me at The Whiskey Whistler. Ray has been coming into the bakery for the last month, asking me to go out with him, and finally I agreed. I sort of had to. No matter how hard I've tried, I can't forget my ex-husband, Nash. Everything I do brings up a memory of us together, and it's driving me crazy. I wanted this divorce. I'm the one that asked for it, and I know I need to move on. "No, actually I've only been here a few years."

He looks at me, waiting for me to continue, but I don't say anything. I moved to Whiskey Run when

Walker and Nash relocated the Ghost Team here, but I don't want to get into all that with Ray.

He shrugs his shoulders. "Uhhhh, okay. They're busy in here tonight. I'm going to go up to the bar and get our drinks. What can I get you?"

I take a deep breath and wish that I could just walk out of here and go home, but I can't. I would like to have a shot–or two–of Blaze Whiskey, which our town is known for, but I don't want to lose my senses. "I'll take a mojito, please."

He smiles and smacks the table in front of us. "Be right back. Save my seat."

I barely refrain from rolling my eyes. I watch him walk away and then around the bar. Since I own the bakery right down the street, I have at one time or another seen or met almost everyone in Whiskey Run. And even though I've only been here a few years, they all treat me as a local, one of them. When I first got to Whiskey Run and Nash was traveling across the world for his job, I was bored. I needed something to do, and since I had worked in my family's bakery since I was little, I opened the Sugar Glaze Bakery. It's probably one of the best things I've done. It's definitely saved me from going stir crazy. I could only take so much sitting at home, waiting for Nash, before I knew I had to do something.

Ray comes back with a tray and sets two drinks in front of me and then a mug of draft beer in front of him. "Here you go... I grabbed you two."

I look at the green fruity-looking drinks in front of me and then up at him. He must have high hopes for how this night is going to play out, but there's no way I'm ready for that. "Thank you, but one's my limit."

He shrugs his shoulders and smiles playfully. "We'll see. The night is young."

I'm already regretting this decision. April, Tara and Becca, the women that work with me at the bakery and are also good friends of mine, have been on me to get back out there. This is the third date I've been on, and I'm about to call it quits. Maybe I'm destined to be on my own forever. There's nothing wrong with it really. I like myself and all, but I know I'm not going to be happy. *If only Nash...*

My hand clenches into a fist, and I slam my eyes shut. *Get it out of your head, Emery. Don't think about him.*

I feel a warm hand on my back. "Are you okay?"

I shake my head back and forth as if I'm trying to get the thoughts out. Truth is, I don't know if I am okay. I don't know if I ever will be. If only...

Damn, there I go again. I force my eyes open and

try to smile at the man that has moved next to me. I hate him touching me. I really do. But I agreed to this date, and he's obviously just trying to be nice. "Yeah, uh, brain freeze that's all."

If he notices that I haven't even taken a drink, he doesn't mention it. His forehead creases. "Ooooh, those are the worst. You know what would make you feel better?"

I know that going home and going to bed will make me feel better. But I don't say it. I just look at him curiously and smile. "What's that?"

He tilts his head out to the dance floor and holds his hand out to me. "A dance?"

The dancing area is full of people doing the latest line dance. I don't want to dance, but I also don't want to ruin this night for Ray. He doesn't deserve my bad mood. Plus, it's a fast song anyway. Instead of putting my hand in his, I slap my hands together as if I'm excited. "Sure, let's go."

I don't wait for him. I turn to go and find an empty spot for us to dance. I smile at him encouragingly as he stops next to me. We have no choice but to start right in on the movements. It's either that or we're going to get knocked into as the dancers shift to one side and then the other. Ray goes the wrong direction and laughs about it, making me smile. The people around us wave or say hello to me, and I force myself to relax and have fun. I'm actually enjoying myself until the music flips over to a slow song.

Ray comes toward me, arms open wide, and it's obvious his intention was a slow dance. I put my hand on his chest to stop him. "Uh, wow, I worked up a thirst. Are you thirsty? I am. Let's go back to the table."

I don't wait for him to answer me. I take off across the room, weaving through couples and back to our table. Our drinks are gone, which is a good thing. I didn't know how I was going to explain how thirsty I was, but I'm not going to drink the alcohol we'd left on the table.

"Oh no, our drinks," Ray says as he approaches the table.

I reach into my crossbody purse and pull out my wallet and hand him a twenty. "Here, next round is on me. I'll take a water this time."

He takes the money. "I'll be right back."

Nash would never...

As soon as the thought enters my mind, I shake my head. *Quit it, Emery. Forget him. It's over. You signed the papers and you are divorced. It's time to move on.*

I fall down into the seat and stare at my hands, missing the wedding ring I once refused to ever take off. I tried giving it back to Nash, but he refused to take it. Now it sits in a jewelry box on top of my dresser, and I'd be lying if I said I didn't look at it every morning.

"Here you go. Water for you and a shot of Jack for me."

Ray no sooner sets my water down than he's throwing back the shot. I watch him as I sip on the water. I don't even ask him about the change from the twenty dollars I gave him. A part of me hopes he keeps it so I feel less guilty when I tell him I'm heading home... alone.

Chapter 3

Nash

I barely get through the door of the Whiskey Whistler and I spot Emery sitting with Ray McCallister. He's a nice enough guy, but he's not good enough for her. Hell, nobody is.

"What's up, Nash? How's it going?"

I briefly look over at Malcolm, the bar manager, and give him a head nod. He must see the concentration on my face because he just shrugs. "Let me know if you need anything."

I slide onto a barstool, my back to the bar top while answering him. "Will do. Thank you, Malcolm."

I stare at Emery. She's the most beautiful woman I've ever seen. She's curvy perfection, and I still can't believe at one point she was mine. At least she was until I completely fucked it up.

Since our divorce, I've been a shell of a man, and even though I know I don't deserve her, I can't continue like this. If I thought she was happy without me, I could probably move on. I'd be miserable, but I'd do it. But she's not happy. She tries to put on a content face, but I know her. I know her better than anyone, and she hasn't moved on either. At least not entirely. By looking at the last few weeks, she's trying to, though, and it hasn't set well with me.

I suck in a breath and rub my hand over my heart. Truth is, since the day she said she wanted a divorce, I've had an ache in my chest that won't go away. I knew I needed to get her back, and I wanted to be able to dedicate one hundred percent to it. The fact that she's started dating has moved up my plans.

Emery is drinking water, and Ray is throwing back another shot. Just since I sat down, he's had two already. I look around the bar briefly and back at Emery. I've been here before, and I know there's one entrance in the front, one in the back, and another through the bathroom windows. Just in my quick glance, there's around forty-five people in the building. I can tell who is packing and who is just here to have a good time. Who's probably going to start a fight and who's leaving with whom. It's all part of the job to know my surroundings. But for the first time, none of that matters. The only thing that matters right now is Emery.

I watch as Ray puts his hand on the back of her chair. Her body stiffens, letting me know she doesn't like it. I know Emery, and I know she can handle herself. I may not have been the best husband, but I sure as hell made sure she knew how to defend herself. I'm out of my seat in an instant when Ray leans over to whisper something in her ear and puts his hand on her shoulder. That's enough. I've had all I can take. Hell, there's no way I can sit here with another man's hands on her.

I stalk toward the other side of the room. I try to calm myself on the way. Not only do I not want to murder someone today, I really don't want to piss Emery off, either. When I get to the table, I pull out the vacant chair and sit on the other side of her. She's staring at me with her mouth hanging open, but her eyes say it all. She's pissed.

I glare right back at her. Ignoring the shmuck sitting on the other side of her, I try to give Emery my best smile. "Hey, honey. Who's this?"

Truth is, I know exactly who Ray is, but none of that matters. He's enemy number one right now.

Emery shrugs Ray's hand off her shoulder, and I nod in approval.

That makes her even madder. She shakes her head, spitting her response to me. "Don't call me that... and don't act like you don't know Ray. You met him in the bakery."

I nod my head, still not looking at Ray. "Right. You're right, I did." I force my eyes off Emery and look at him. I did meet him at the bakery. I thought he was some random guy getting desserts. I had no idea he was trying to pick up my wife. He's obviously had more to drink than I thought. His eyes are glassy, and he's looking at me almost cocky like. I smirk at him. "So, Ray. Want to tell me why you're touching my wife?"

Ray's mouth drops open, and he stares between Emery and me. Emery gasps and grabs me by the arm. "We're not married." She looks at Ray. "We're not married. He's my ex-husband." She stands up from the table and pulls on my arm. "Ray, can you give us a minute?" She doesn't wait for him to respond. She starts tugging me toward the exit. "You! Come with me."

I go with her but make sure to give a lethal glare

toward Ray. I can tell exactly what he was hoping was going to happen tonight, and it's not going to. Emery can get mad at me all she wants.

As soon as we get outside, she lets go of me, and I follow her to the edge of the building. She turns, crossing her arms over her chest. "What do you think you're doing?"

I sigh. This is not how I wanted this to play out. The meeting with the rest of the Ghost Team this afternoon went smoothly, but the men were all surprised, to say the least. Did I think I could come here and tell her I'm stepping back from the business and everything was going to be okay? I should have known better... and I definitely shouldn't have started this by pissing her off. "Look, I'm sorry. I came to—"

She doesn't let me finish. She throws her hands in the air. "You came to interfere. For months now, you've shown up everywhere I am. I've seen you more since the divorce than I did when we were married. Nash... this has to stop."

I shake my head. "I can't. I'm sorry, Emery, but I can't let you go."

She looks so sad. "You already did. You signed the papers."

I reach for her, but she draws back, and I let my

hands fall to my side. "I didn't want to sign them, but you were so mad, so upset... I couldn't stand seeing you like that. I had a mission."

She rolls her eyes. "You always have a mission."

Tell her you're stepping back. Now's your opening. But I open my mouth and close it real quick. She's too mad, she's not going to listen, and even if she does, she's not going to care. I fist my hands at my side. "I know I was gone a lot..."

She laughs out loud, but I continue. "I know I did a lot of things wrong, things I regret."

She looks almost scared as she searches my face. "I don't wanna hear it..."

I take a step toward her. "You need to hear it, Emery. I know I messed up, but I want to fix it. I can't go on like this. We can't go on like this."

She cocks her shapely hip out and puts her hand on it. "Why? Why do you care now? All this time, I was yours, Nash. You had me and never had the time for me. Now I'm dating and putting myself out there and you decide you want me."

I clench my eyes, count to three, and open them. "I've always wanted you. I didn't deserve you. I still don't. But I love you, Emery. I always have and I always will."

She wants to believe me. The hope is evident in her face that she wants to. But just as soon as her face starts to soften, her guard comes back up. "No!"

"No? What do you mean, no?"

She's shaking her head, and her hand trembles as she pushes a piece of hair off her face. "I mean, no, Nash. I can't go through this again. All the traveling..."

I start to interrupt her and tell her that I'm not traveling anymore, but she doesn't let me. She holds her hand up. "Stop. Let me finish. All the traveling, and even when you were here you were never HERE. And then the women... I can't."

"Women? What women? What the hell are you talking about, Emery?"

She grabs the strap of the purse that's hanging across her body. Her knuckles are white from how tight she's holding it. "I'm not going to spell it out for you. The other women. I'm not stupid to believe that you were gone all that time and..." She holds her hand up and starts backing away. "You know what? Forget it. I'm not getting into this now. It's over, Nash. We're over."

I let her go. My whole body is vibrating in anger. How can she even think I would ever betray her? I would never. From the day I met her, I haven't looked at another woman. Even since the divorce, I haven't bothered. I know that there's only one woman for me, and unfortunately, I'm starting to realize that she may not want anything to do with me.

Chapter 4

Emery

I almost go back into the Whiskey Whistler, but as I feel the wetness on my cheeks, I change my mind. I go past the door and walk down the block toward my car. I probably should feel bad or guilty for the way that I just left Ray with no explanation, but I can't seem to make myself care right now. All this time has gone by, I finally decide to try and start dating again, and now Nash pulls this. He can't pull a stunt like that just because he doesn't want me to date someone.

My car is parked only a block away, and I get in and slam the door shut and lay my head on the steering wheel. A deep agony fills me. It's the same hurt I've felt since I mentioned the word divorce, but it's even more intense.

I know it sounds foolish, but a part of me wants to walk back to where I left Nash standing. Every part of my being tells me that he is not the type to cheat. I know he's not, but still there's that little glimmer of doubt that has rocked my insecurities since he agreed to the divorce. Why else would he have agreed like he did? But I shouldn't have thrown it in his face. Not like that. Through everything– even the divorce–he has gone out of his way to be nice to me. He left me the house, pays an alimony that is way too much, and even though I denied it, he still sends it to my bank account each month. And how do I repay him? By accusing him of cheating when I'm really not sure that's what happened.

I start the car and drive down the street toward my big, empty house. It's the same one that I lived in when Nash and I were married, and it's definitely too big, but I don't have the strength to sell it. I know it sounds stupid, but it's like the very last thing that I have that was part of Nash's and my life together. I can't part with it.

I get a block down the street, and there are headlights in my rearview mirror. I don't even get worried as the lights shine in my eyes. I know exactly who it is. Since the divorce, anytime I drive at night, it's been Nash that has followed me home. More and more lately. It's like when we were married he was never in town, and now he's here all the time. I wasn't lying when I told him that I feel like I see him more now that we're divorced than when we were married. It's the truth. If he had given me just half the attention he gives me now, we probably could have worked things out. I don't know what is going on with him, but I won't let myself get into a situation to get hurt again. I don't think I could survive it.

When I pull into the driveway, Nash's Suburban stops at the end of the driveway. I push the button to open the garage and pull in. As soon as I'm in, I push the button again to close the garage doors, and I watch as Nash's SUV disappears in the rearview mirror. I get out of the car and walk into the house, turning off the security system as I walk through the door. That's one thing that he always stressed as important. He always wanted to make sure I was safe. There were so many times that I felt he was trying to be controlling and maybe too possessive, but he promised me it was only because he wanted me protected. It wasn't until I realized exactly how dangerous his job really was that I discovered his need to keep me safe was the truth.

I step out of my shoes and stop at the entryway,

picking up the mail that the mailman had put through the slot of the door. I leaf through the envelopes, and there's one that calls out to me. I drop all of the other letters on the table and stare at the official-looking white envelope. In big bold letters on the upper lefthand side is the name of the adoption agency that I recently applied to. I hurriedly open the envelope, unfolding the paper that was inside and scan the words in front of me. "I'm sorry, but at this time we are unable to process your application. Please reach out to us in the future when your circumstances have changed."

I let my hands fall, and the letter smacks against my leg. Circumstances? I shake my head in disbelief. There are so many kids in this world that need somebody to love them. I could do that, but time after time, I get denied because I am a single woman.

I had all of these dreams when I was married to Nash. He never believed that he could be a good father, but I always thought I would be able to change his mind. When we got married, I thought it was going to be forever. At least I wanted it to be. I had no idea how many days, nights, weeks, months I would go without even seeing him. Sometimes not even knowing where he was at in this world. And then when he was home, he was still thinking about work. I know what he does is important, and I would never want him to give that up, but I guess I just wanted more for us.

I walk into my home office and go straight to the board I have hanging on my wall. With a black marker, I scratch off the name of the adoption agency that just sent me the rejection letter. There's two more on the list I have not heard back from yet. I haven't given up all hope yet. I can't. I know that there is a child out there that needs me, and I'm not going to let anything stop me from doing this. It would've been easier with Nash as my husband. Heck, that's what I always wanted, but somehow I have to force myself to change my dreams a little, even if I don't really want to.

Chapter 5

Nash

I'm not on my game. This whole day, I've felt off. Usually, I trust my gut and put myself on high alert, but since my talk with Emery the other night, I'm sure it's that. Emery is all I've thought about.

I've wanted to talk to her, but I haven't trusted myself. I would never hurt Emery, but I might say things I shouldn't. I still can't believe that she thinks I'm interested in another woman or that I would cheat on her. Fuck, even now that we're divorced, I couldn't look at another woman because to me, it would be cheating. I have followed her home. I've sat outside the bakery and waited for her to go in or to come out at night. I know she sees me, but she's acting like she doesn't. But that's fine. I need to cool off a little bit more before I talk to her.

Second Chance Love

I've been working all morning, working on getting Colt caught up on files and cases. We've gone over procedures until he can recite them in his sleep. He's ready. Hell, he was born for this.

I'm leaving the compound when I notice the car on the side of the road. I'm on my way to Sugar Glaze, hoping to see Emery before she walks into the shop, but when I notice the lone woman standing at the open hood, I ease my Suburban to the side of the road and turn on my hazard lights.

As I walk up to her car, she looks at me worriedly. "Thanks for stopping."

I smile at her, just so she knows I'm not some kind of psycho. "No problem. What's wrong?"

She sniffs, and I notice the bruise on her face. Instantly, my blood starts to boil. "Uh, it just started sputtering, and smoke started coming out from the hood."

I lean down to look at the car when I hear the squeal of tires. I no sooner lift my head than there's a car stopping next to us in the middle of the road. "You cheatin' bitch, is this the man you're leaving me for?"

It doesn't register with me that he has a gun until it's too late. He gets off a shot, and I'm shoving the woman to the ground on the other side of the vehicle.

I feel the impact of the bullet in my arm. Stumbling on the uneven ground has me falling face first to the cement, and I hit hard metal on the way down.

Dazed and disoriented, I hear screaming from the woman and know I need to act fast or we'll both be done. I pull the 380 from my belt holster and blink, trying to clear my vision. I shake my head, but that doesn't seem to help because pain shoots behind my eyes.

I get to my knees, and I can tell the woman is struggling as the man is trying to grab her. I squint my eyes, and the picture before me comes clearer. I take the shot before I can second-guess myself, and the man falls. I crawl toward him and pocket his gun. The woman falls to the ground, crying, but I can't focus on that right now. I can't seem to focus on anything. I pull my phone from my pocket.

I use voice command. "Call Walker."

When I hear Walker's voice, I mutter the word "help" before everything goes black.

I don't remember anything after that. Nothing. I know Walker will find me since everyone with the Ghost Team has tracking on our phones. I feel myself drifting in and out of consciousness, the voices and sirens, but no matter how hard I try, I can't seem to wake from the black hole I'm in.

It's not until I'm being rolled down a hall of what I assume is Jasper Hospital when everything starts to come into focus. The overhead lights seem as if they're blaring, and I can hear Walker, almost breathless as he walks next to me.

"Walker! Walker!"

"I'm here, brother. You're going to be okay. The woman is fine."

I can hear the pain and yearning in my voice as I plead to him. "Emery. I need Emery."

"I got you, brother. I'll make the call. The bullet took a chunk out of your arm, but they can sew it, no surgery. But they need to check your head. I'll have Emery here when you get out."

I groan my response. Everything seems to come into super focus and then get blurry again. I have no choice but to close my eyes and let the darkness seep in. I feel a twinge in my arm and I know they're sewing me up.

Then I feel as if I'm in a tunnel, and I'm assuming they're doing more tests. I let my thoughts wander, and it isn't long before I'm thinking of Emery. My thoughts always go to her, and I shouldn't expect anything different even though everything is grainy. I swear I feel as if I can reach out and touch her as the memory starts to play out in my head.

It was the first time we met, and it was the day my whole life changed.

I was at the bar with Walker and a few of the other guys. We were just getting started with the Ghost Team, and then we were located in Texas. Emery and her friends walked into the bar, and I could feel my heart stop. Literally, it stopped beating for a few seconds. I couldn't breathe or anything. All I did was stare.

She's still the most beautiful woman I've ever met. I tried to pay attention to the guys talking, but I couldn't take my eyes off Emery. She saw me too. She'd look at me and then glance away real quick when she noticed me watching her.

I was working up the courage to go and talk to her when the song changed on the juke box, and she and all her friends squealed and jumped up from their seats. The song was going on about *this is how we do it,* and she knew it word for word. She danced and laughed and shook her ass as if she didn't have a care in the world. She was way out of my league, but I couldn't take my eyes off her.

And it seems, no one else in the bar could either.

As soon as the song was over, she and her friends

were laughing and talking, waiting for the next song when a man came toward her. I was up in an instant, and so were Walker and the rest of the guys. It sort of comes with the business to be on high alert and ready for anything. I held my hand up to them. "I got this. I'll be back."

I stalked across the room, and by the time I got close, the stranger had his hand wrapped around Emery's elbow. My hands were fisted at my sides, but that was the only tell I was pissed. I didn't want to risk scaring her off. "Sorry I'm late, sweetie."

I reached out to Emery, and she came to me instantly. I held my arms open, and she stepped close to me. I put one arm around her waist and pulled her soft body against mine.

The man was big and obviously stupid. "Hey, she was just about to dance with me."

I had been hoping to avoid any confrontation, but if this was what it came down to, fine. I looked down into the green eyes of the woman in my arms. She pressed one hand to my chest, and I brought up one hand to hold it there. Her palm spread out right over my heart. Huskily, I asked her, "You want to dance with him?"

I held my breath because I didn't know what I'd do if she said yes. I didn't think I could let her go.

She shook her head side to side, and I finally started to breathe easier. I forced my gaze off her and to the man, who was still standing there. "The lady doesn't want to dance with you."

The man was pissed. His cheeks were ruddy, and I was sure he was embarrassed because all eyes in the bar were on us. It's times like this, where egos are on the line, that men sometimes do stupid things. I didn't take my eyes off him. He seemed to stand up straighter and puffed his chest out. I was ready for the attack when I heard four chairs behind me make a loud grinding sound across the floor. I didn't even have to look. I knew it was Walker and the guys, ready to come to my defense if need be. The man must have noticed them because he shrugged his shoulders, and with one last menacing look, he walked away.

Emery sighed loudly beside me. "Wow. Uh, thank you for that."

Her friends were still standing off to the side, watching us. Emery tried to pull her hand away, but I didn't let go. "You're welcome. Can I ask you... two things?"

She looked at her friends, and they were all encouraging her. She looked back up at me. "Yes."

I turned so we were facing each other. "What's your name?"

"Emery. What's yours?"

"Hunter. But everyone calls me Nash."

She swallowed. "Nash, what's your second question?"

"Emery, do you want to dance with me?"

She let out a small gasp and stuttered, "But, uh, there's no music."

Right then, the jukebox started playing a slow song. I looked over and Walker was leaning against it. I never thought Walker was a romantic type of guy, but I'd take all the help I could get.

"What about now?" I asked her, not wanting to pressure her but hoping and praying she wouldn't say no either.

"Sure, I'd love to dance with you."

I pulled her to me, afraid she'd change her mind. I'd never been good with women, and I was a blunt person, but with her I didn't want to screw this up. I couldn't think of anything but how Emery felt in my arms. I was committing it all to memory, the smell of her, the way her long hair brushed against my arm as we swayed back and forth, the way her body seemed to melt into mine. Everything.

She leaned her head back and looked up at me.

"So is this your thing? You go bar to bar and save women that need help?"

I laughed. "No, it's not my thing. I was just lucky today, I guess."

She looked over at the table where my friends were. "Are you all in the military?"

I shrugged, tightening my hold on her. "Something like that." There was no way I could explain it to her now, and I knew I didn't want to. There was no way I wanted to give her any reason to walk away from me. "Tell me about you."

She shrugged her shoulders. "What do you want to know?"

"Everything," I insisted.

The music continued, a soft ballad of love everlasting, and I'd never wanted a song to last forever in my life. "Well, let's see. My name is Emery Mason, and I'm twenty-three years old. I have worked in my parents' bakery since I was little. I love to bake–as you can see."

She gestured toward her body and rolled her eyes. Fuck, I wondered, did she think she was fat? She was perfect. She was younger than me by about ten years, but I didn't even care. "You're perfect the way you are."

She cleared her throat. "So do you live here, in Houston?"

"For now. I travel a lot... for my job."

She nodded, looking back over at the guys, no doubt thinking that I was military. She looked up at me with a glint in her eye. "That's too bad.... I think I would have liked getting to know you."

I brought my hand up and cupped the side of her neck. "Oh honey, you're definitely going to get to know me."

She was almost breathless and panting when she asked, "Why?"

I leaned down until our lips were not even an inch apart. I could feel her warm breath on my cheek, and I watched as her eyes darkened, and her heart seemed to be racing in her chest. "Why? Because you're going to be my wife."

She gasped then, and I pressed my lips to hers. She started to pull away, but I deepened the kiss. Our lips meshed in perfect harmony as her body softened against mine. I knew she could feel my desire pushed against her belly, but she didn't seem to care. She pressed into me, trying to get as close as she could.

She pulled back, almost dazed, but smiling. "How about a date first?"

She felt it. I knew she did. There was something between us, something stronger than I'd ever felt. I pressed my forehead to hers. "Yeah, I'm good with that."

"Mr. Nash! Can you hear me?"

I try to ignore the voice calling out to me. I hate that someone is interrupting my memory, but I know I have to let it go. The sooner I wake up, the sooner I'll get to see Emery. Walker promised he'd get her here, and I know she'll come. I can't let myself think otherwise.

Chapter 6

Emery

I have to get to him. That's all I can think about as I ride in the back seat of Lucas' truck next to Becca. The call I got from Walker telling me that Nash had been shot had me falling to the ground in anguish. Walker had told me that he would come and get me, but I made him promise to stay with Nash, I would get there as soon as I could. Becca is one of my best friends, and she works at my bakery. I knew she hadn't got to work yet and she would take me into Jasper with no questions asked. I wasn't thinking about interrupting her time with her new boyfriend, Lucas, though.

Lucas is flying toward Jasper, and my hands are holding tightly on to one another in my lap. Becca has her arm around me trying to soothe me, but nothing is going to calm me until I have Nash in my sight, and I know that he is going to be okay. The road to Jasper normally takes 30 minutes, but it seems to fly by because before I know it, Lucas is dropping us off at the front door of the emergency room of Jasper Hospital.

I'm wiping at the tears that won't stop falling from my eyes as I all but run into the waiting room. I spot Walker and all of the guys, and Walker opens his arms to me. I run to him and hold on tightly. "Tell me he's okay. Tell me that Nash is going to be okay."

I'm holding on to the front of his shirt, pleading with him to make promises to me that he may not be able to keep. "He's fine, Emery. He's asking for you, he needs to see you."

I start to walk away and look over at Becca. She shakes her head. "Go, I'll be here."

I walk with Walker down the hallway and ask him curiously, "What happened? How did he get shot?"

There are so many things I don't know about the Ghost Team, and a lot of it they can't give you answers to. I don't know how many times things happened that Nash came home with bruises and cuts and things like that and I couldn't ask any questions. So I probably shouldn't be asking now, but I'm surprised when Walker answers me, "A woman had broken down on the highway, and Nash stopped to help her with her car. The woman's boyfriend stopped and was mad. I guess he had just beaten her up as she was leaving. He got a shot off at Nash, but it grazed his arm. They're more worried about his head because he hit the bumper going down."

My hand tightens around Walker's. "But is he going to be okay?"

He nods as we stop outside of a door. There are doctors and nurses walking all around us, but I don't pay attention to any of them. My eyes are glued to Walker, wanting to make sure that he's telling me the truth.

"The doctors say that head injuries are the worst, but it's a good thing that he remembers you and the rest of us."

I nod. "Good, that's good, right?"

He nods reassuringly. "Yeah, honey, that's good."

On the way to the hospital, I thought about our fight the other night and all the horrible things that I accused him of. We haven't talked since, even though I know he's been around watching me like he normally does. I take a deep breath, and Walker looks at me with his hand on the door. "Are you ready?"

I can feel by the way Walker is looking at me that it's a loaded question. He's not asking me if I'm just ready to walk into a hospital room to check on an old friend; he's wanting to know if I'm ready for more. Truth is, I don't know if I am or not, but I know that I won't leave here until I know that Nash is okay. I nod my head and sob, "I'm ready."

We walk into the room, and Nash's head is lolling to the side. From where I'm standing, he looks okay, his color is a little off, and the soft beep of the machine standing next to him is annoying, but at least he's breathing... at least he's in one piece.

Walker leans down and whispers to me so as not to disturb Nash, "I'm going to give you all some time, okay?"

Without even looking at him, I nod and walk over toward the bed. I hear the door as it closes behind him, but I can't take my eyes off Nash. Even lying there with machines hooked up to him, he's the most handsome man I've ever met. I debate whether I should touch him or talk to him, but I don't debate long. The need to touch him and feel him again is intense. I reach out and touch my finger along the back of his hand. It's just a gentle touch, but it's enough.

Nash's eyes open, and he blinks at me, over and over as if he doesn't believe what he's seeing. "You came," he says, surprised.

I can't hold back the sob, and I know I'm blubbering like an idiot, but I nod my head. "Yeah, I came, of course I came."

I can't stop the tears this time, and he lifts his hand and wraps it around my wrist, pulling me toward him. I go to him willingly, at least until I see the grimace on his face. "I'll hurt you."

He stops pulling, but he doesn't release me. He looks me square in the eye. "You won't hurt me, Emery. If I could just hold you one more time, you would help me, you would make me feel better."

I could never resist Nash before, and I'm learning that I can't now either. I go to him and lie down on the side of the bed next to him. His arm is around my back, and my hand goes to his chest. There are wires everywhere, but neither one of us seems to care. I rest my head on his shoulder, and when I do, he lets out a long, deep, satisfying breath as if the weight of the world has been on his shoulders and now he's free.

We lie there for I don't know how long, but I

know I have to say what's on my mind. "I'm sorry about the other night, what I said to you."

He tucks his chin against the top of my head. "You don't owe me an apology. I have so many regrets, Emery." I can hear the weight of those regrets in his voice. *Does he regret marrying me or even meeting me?*

He must feel me stiffen because his next words soothe me. "I don't regret us, so don't think that. And honey, I need to tell you now, I think that you've already worked it out, but you need to know that I've never looked at another woman, not since the day that I met you in that bar in Texas. You are the only woman for me."

I shake my head but refuse to look him in the eye. "I didn't really believe that you had cheated on me, Nash. Maybe I wanted to let myself believe it so that this could be easier."

He doesn't say anything, so I have to ask, "What are your regrets?"

His arms tighten around me. "I regret leaving you all the time. I regret that we didn't have kids. I regret —" But I don't let him finish.

I rear back, and this time I look him in the eye. "I didn't think you wanted kids."

He shakes his head. "I didn't. I had a fucked-up

childhood, and I never wanted to mess up some kid by being a shitty father. But now I'd give anything to have had a baby with you."

He looks at me intensely, straight in the eye as if he's searching my face trying to read what's on my mind. "Why? Do you want a baby?"

Chapter 7

Nash

She's staring at me in surprise, and for the first time since she walked in the room, she's no longer crying. I patiently wait for her to answer my question. Obviously, it's an important one by the way that her body is pulled tight, and she seems to have stopped breathing. I brush the hair off the side of her face and tuck it behind her ear.

"Tell me, do you want a baby?"

She nods without blinking. "You know I do, Nash. I've always wanted a baby."

I take in a deep breath. She's right. I knew she wanted kids, but I was too involved with thinking I could save the world instead of taking care of her wants and her needs. Knowing that and letting it finally sink in hits me right in the gut. I should have known how important it was to her to have a child. She will make a great mother. I should have let my past stay in the past. And yeah, I'm worried about being a shitty father, but if I have Emery by my side, I know she won't let me.

I'm fighting off the pain meds, but I can feel the grogginess starting to set in. I need to stay alert for this conversation. She tries to sit up a little, but I don't let her go far. She pats me on the chest. "Tell me... tell me why you want to have kids."

I let my head fall back on the pillow, and I close my eyes. I'm not someone that talks about my feelings. I never have been, but I know I have to learn to open up If I want any kind of future with Emery.

With my eyes closed, I tell her exactly what I'm thinking. "I never knew what love was until I met you, Emery. I'd be lying if I didn't say I was scared... hell, I'm scared to death of being a father. But only because I don't want to screw it up. I would love to have a child knowing that it's a part of us." I open my eyes and stare at her. "But most importantly, I want a child because I want to be tied to you forever, Emery. I know that I have fucked up in the past, and I know that you're looking at me right now like I'm not the best dad material, but I can do better. I can be better."

She must see the anguish on my face. She pushes the hair off my forehead and cups my cheek. There's still so much I need to tell her. "We don't need to talk about this now, Nash. You've been shot. You have a head injury. The best thing for you right now is to rest."

I shake my head. I know what she's saying is right, but still I can't let this moment pass by. "Honey, this is the first time that I've gotten you to listen to me that you haven't wanted to either slap me or run away. I need to use my time wisely."

She smirks at me as if I'm joking, but I'm not. For months, she's avoided me, but she shakes her head, rolling her eyes. I blink as the light seems to mess with my vision. She looks at the light and then back at me. "Do you want me to turn that off?"

I shake my head instantly. "No."

"Nash, your head would probably feel better if it was darker in here."

I shrug my shoulders. "I'll deal with the pain. I don't want to let you up from here."

She's surprised by that, and her face softens as she looks at me. "What if I promise to just get up and turn the light off and come right back?"

I bring one hand up and cover part of my eyes to

shield it from the light, wanting to be able to look at her directly. "You promise?"

She nods, patting my chest. "I promise."

I let her get out of the bed and watch as she walks over to the door. It's like I'm holding my breath, hoping that she doesn't run from me. I don't know what I'll do if she walks out. Probably try and follow her and fall on my ass in the process. But she doesn't run. She flips the light switch and walks back over to me, taking off her cross-body purse and putting it on the table next to the bed. She's about to crawl back in beside me when she looks at my arm. "Nash, it's this arm. I was lying on this arm that you were just shot in. Why didn't you say anything? I know it had to hurt."

"Honey, there's no way I was going to do anything that would stop you from lying in my arms."

She starts to walk away, and I reach for her, but she just keeps going. "I'm just going to the other side."

I nod and watch her walk around to the other side of the bed. She climbs up into the bed and tries to lie on her side, away from me. It's a small bed, and I take up a lot of the room, but I don't even want an inch between us.

The grogginess is starting to take over, but I'm not going to let it win until I know I have her firmly in my arms and she plans to stay there. "Closer," I grunt at her.

She scoots closer, and I put my arm around her and hold her tight. "I'm so sleepy, Emery."

She looks at me worriedly. "I didn't even ask. What did the doctors say? Are you even allowed to sleep?"

I yawn loudly. "It's just a concussion. No brain bleeds or anything. I just have to wake up every hour. Don't worry. The nurses will be in to wake me up, I'm sure."

"Oh, Nash," she says worriedly. "I'm so glad that you're okay. I don't know what I would do..." She stops suddenly as if she's giving away too much. But I didn't miss it. She doesn't want me to know that she still feels something for me, but her words seem to give me hope. The truth is we are still bound together. She still loves me just as I still love her. Somehow, some way we have to find a way to make this work. I won't let anything else happen.

I mutter to her, "Promise me that you won't leave me."

I wait to hear her response. "I promise," she says.

And it's only then with her held tightly in my arms and the promise that she won't leave me that I finally let myself fall to sleep.

Chapter 8

Emery

I snuggle deeper into the hard warmth that is surrounding me. Something is drawing me awake, but I'm fighting it. I don't want to lose the comfort I'm feeling right now. I can't remember waking up so rested. There's an irritating beep, beep, beep, but I'm able to block it out. It isn't until I hear voices that I come fully alert. I blink as I open my eyes and see that I'm lying in bed with Nash, and then it all comes back to me. The doctor is talking, and I'm embarrassed to be found lying in the bed with a patient that has been shot. I'm sure this is against some kind of rules or something.

I struggle to get up, but Nash holds on to me tightly. "Stay, honey."

I do as he asks so I don't make a scene, and the

doctor continues. "The arm should heal nicely, but we're going to go ahead and put you on some antibiotics and something for the pain. The head injury is most worrisome, but I know this is not your first concussion. You'll need someone to make sure that you wake up every hour and that someone stays with you."

Nash's forehead creases, and frustration is laced in every word he mutters. "I don't need a babysitter."

I look at him. He's one of the strongest men I know, and he hates to ask for help. He's always been this way. A lot of it is the way he grew up. He never had anyone. Since he was a young child, he's had to do everything on his own. Even when we were married, he never would let me share in things that bothered him. He just wanted to take care of it himself. Maybe that was one of our problems. I let him do that.

I put my hand on his chest and crawl it up around his neck. "I'll stay with you. I can take care of you."

He looks at me, surprised, but he nods and then looks at the doctor. "Okay. What else?"

"That's it. You'll need to follow up with your primary care doctor next week. If you have any bad headaches or any changes with your vision or anything, you'll need to come back in, though. Immediately."

"Okay. I can do that."

The doctor holds his clipboard down at his side. He looks at me and then back at Nash. "Can I speak freely?"

"Yes," Nash says as he spans his hand across my hip. Does he think the doctor is going to say something that will make me run? I hate to admit it, but there's no way I'm leaving him now. Not until I know he's really going to be fine. Even then it will be hard letting him go again.

The doctor pulls his clipboard up and starts to read from it. "You're lucky, Nash. Five concussions, shot twice, broken ribs, and dislocated shoulder... all of that in the last year. If I didn't know better, I would think you have a death wish."

I gasp, and my mouth falls open as I stare at Nash. He won't look at me, though. He grunts at the doctor instead, "I don't have a death wish. When can I get out of here?"

The doctor opens his mouth and closes it again. Finally, he shakes his head. "Fine. I'll get your discharge papers, and we should get you out of here within an hour."

Nash nods. "Okay. Thanks, Doc."

The doctor walks out the door, and Nash looks at me. "Are you sure you're okay with this? What about the bakery?"

My eyes widen. "The bakery? Nash, you know the girls can handle the bakery without me. You're more important."

He looks surprised and then he clenches his eyes closed as if he just thought of something painful. I put my hand on his cheek. "Are you okay? Is your head hurting?"

He leans his face into my hand as if he is yearning for my touch. When he opens his eyes, I swear there's wetness there. "No, my head's not hurting. You're too good to me, Emery. You always have been. I have so much to make up to you."

I smile and shake my head. "No way, Nash. None of that. We're not going to get into that right now. Let's get you better first." I point my finger into his chest. "But I promise you this. I'm not forgetting what the doctor just said. You have a lot of explaining to do."

He doesn't deny it or try to get out of it. He grabs on to my hand and brings it up to lay over his heart. He holds it there, and I can feel it beating wildly under my palm. I don't know how, but already, I feel closer to him than in all our years of marriage. He seems to want to open up to me, but I'm not sure he knows how. I clear my throat. "The planner in me is already working things out in my head. Let's get you settled at your house and then I'll run home and pack a bag real quick."

He shakes his head, interrupting me. "No, I can stay at your house. That way, you'll be close to the bakery in case you do need to go in and check on things."

I rear back, surprised. "But you'll be farther from your office."

He shrugs like it doesn't matter. "It'll be fine. I have things covered."

I watch him, waiting. There's something that he's not telling me. I know Nash well enough to know that every thought he has is about a case he's working on or a mission or somebody else with the Ghost Team. But he surprises me by acting as if it's no big deal that he may be off of work for a while.

I lean against him. "Are you sure? I don't want you to have to drive to the compound from my house when yours is closer. I know you're probably not allowed to drive anyway, but I also know that there's no stopping you once you decide to do something."

He shakes his head. "I'm not going to the compound. I'm going to go to our house and rest."

I act like I don't hear him call it our house and deciding that I better not push it, I change the subject. "Okay, then how are we going to get to the house?"

"Hand me my phone, Emery."

I reach to the table next to the bed, unplug his phone, and hand it to him. I lean over and grab my purse, pulling my phone out too. I completely forgot about Becca. She's probably freaking out right now.

He starts typing into his. "I'm going to text Walker. He'll have someone pack up my things and come and pick us up and take us home." He looks up from his typing. "Where's your car? Do I need to get somebody to bring it somewhere?"

I shake my head. "No, I was a mess when I got the call. I had Becca and her new boyfriend bring me here."

I open my messaging app to text Becca, but I see a text from her. She sent me a picture of Nash and me in the hospital bed, and I can't look away. We look cozy and dare I say happy. I read the message. "You looked all right and Walker said Nash was going to be fine now. I left, but call me when you want to come home and I'll come get you. Love you."

I text her back. "He's getting out today. He's staying at my house and we have a ride. I'll explain later. Thank you and Lucas again for bringing me here. Love you."

I put my phone down and watch as Nash pushes the button on the phone to send the text and then lays it down in his lap. "I'm sorry for everything that I've put you through, Emery."

I lift my shoulder and shrug. "It's not your fault that you were shot."

"I don't mean this. I mean everything. There's so many things I need to apologize to you for. There's so many things I need to make up to you."

I lean my head down on his shoulder because the look he's giving me is way too intense. Part of me knows that I need to keep my guard up or else I'm going to be hurt again. "It's fine, Nash. I know you never meant to hurt me. All that matters now is that you're going to be okay."

He puts his lips to my forehead and kisses me there. When he pulls back, his voice is just a whisper. "We are going to be okay."

My heart flipflops in my chest. I wish that was the truth.

Chapter 9

Nash

I'm lying back in the recliner and trying not to eavesdrop on Emery and her girlfriends in the kitchen.

Walker picked up Emery and me from the hospital and helped us get settled at the house. Emery's been going crazy around here trying to get everything situated, and she won't let me help at all. I hear a burst of laughter from the kitchen, and then all of a sudden it stops, and Emery pokes her head out, looking at me. "Are you okay? Do you need anything? I'm warming up the chocolate croissants that you like."

It's on the tip of my tongue to ask her to come and sit with me, but I know there'll be plenty of time for that later. Tara, April, and Becca are her best friends, and I know that with everything going on, she needs them right now, so I'm not going to ruin that. "No, honey, I'm good. Take your time. I'll stay right here. I promise."

Her eyes widen, but she nods her head and disappears back into the kitchen. I know she's confused by my behavior. I've never been one to do what I've been told to do, so my actions are probably a surprise for her. She probably expected to look out here and find me gone or something.

A few minutes go by, and Emery and her friends all come out of the kitchen. Emery brings me the chocolate croissants and sits down on the couch. She's too far from me, but I'm not going to say anything about it now. I hold my plate up to the women. "Thank you for this!"

Becca responds first. "We know they're your favorite."

And then Becca chimes in. "Yeah, you all let us know if you need anything. One of us can bring whatever you need."

I nod and so does Emery. Tara hangs back and walks up to my chair, holding her fist out to me. I raise my hand and fist-bump her, and she smiles brightly. "I was rooting for you this whole time." She looks toward Emery and then back at me. "Don't fuck it up."

I laugh. "I won't," I promise her.

She nods, and then the three ladies walk out. As soon as the door closes behind them, I'm pushing the lever down on the chair to put my feet down.

Emery jumps up. "What is it? What do you need?"

But I continue standing up, holding the plate of croissants. I walk over toward the couch. "I just want to sit next to you."

She looks at the recliner and back to me. "But you love that recliner. That was always YOUR seat."

I sit down next to her, so close that our legs are touching, and I shrug and hold the plate of croissants up to her. "I'd rather be closer to you. Do you want one?"

She shakes her head side to side, and I take a big bite of the chocolate croissant, moaning around the flavors. Emery pulls her feet up underneath of her, crosses her arms over her chest, and leans back in the cushions. I finish off the croissant and set the plate on the coffee table and lean back on the couch. "Am I going to bore you to death?"

She says, "No. I like this, actually. I like to stay home."

I clear my throat. "I hate to ask the question, but I know I need to. Have you been dating a lot?"

She barks out a laugh. "Like you don't know. I think that you've shown up at every one I've been on."

I should probably be embarrassed, but I'm not. I've been jealous, and I won't apologize for it. I shrug my shoulders. "I'm not going to apologize for ruining your one the other night. Ray's an asshole."

She picks up the remote for the television and turns it on it. "It wasn't a big deal. I don't think we hit it off anyway."

I lean up and look at her intensely. "Have you gone on a date with someone that you like or want to get to know better?"

She looks at me out the side of her eye and lets out a breath. It's obvious that she doesn't want to admit it, but finally she answers me. "No. I actually hate dating. The girls have been worried about me, though. And it worked out for Becca."

I reach over and lay the back of my hand on her thigh. My palm is up, and my fingers are spread open. "I don't want you to date anyone."

"Nash," she starts, but I don't let her finish.

"No, hear me out. I know I fucked up, and I know that I'm never going to make it completely right, but I need you to give me a chance to explain things."

She clenches her eyes shut, and when she opens them, I can see the fierce determination on her face. "While you're here, Nash, I won't date anyone else, or I won't go on any more dates, but you can't ask more than that."

She's right, and I know I need to take this one step at a time. I flex my fingers, still palm up. "Will you hold my hand?"

There's frustration laced in her voice. "Why?"

She seems so confused, and I can't blame her. I know I've done a number on her, and I need to come clean. But I also know that I can't do that until she's willing to listen. "Because I want to be close to you. I need to feel you. And if all I can get is to hold your hand, then I'll take it."

She uncrosses her arms from her chest and then places her hand over mine. I lace our fingers together and hold on to her tightly. It's so simple, holding hands, but right now it's one step in the right direction. I just can't fuck it up again. I won't let myself.

Chapter 10

Emery

I'm exhausted, and I know he is too. We haven't done a lot. I only got up to fix him a sandwich and to use the bathroom. The rest of the time, we've sat next to each other on the couch, holding hands. I thought it would be awkward and uncomfortable, but it wasn't. We watched TV and laughed with the lights turned down low. But there's no more putting it off. I know he needs his rest.

"I'm going to go on to bed," I tell him. "I have everything set up upstairs."

He turns off the television with the remote. "Me too. I'm exhausted."

He goes to lock the doors, but I stop him. "I've already double-checked. Everything is locked up and the alarm is set."

He nods approvingly and follows behind me up the stairs. I can feel his gaze burning into my body, and I try not to let it affect me. I take a deep breath as I walk into our bedroom. I could have easily set him up in one of the guest rooms, but I thought he would be more comfortable here. I turn down the bed and then disappear into the bathroom without another word. My gown and robe are hanging on the back of the door, and I get ready for bed. When I come out, he is already lying down, and the only light in the room is the lamp on the nightstand.

I bypass the bed and go to the closet, pulling out a blanket from the top shelf. We have a large chair in the corner of the room, and that's where I plan on sleeping. I thought about just sleeping in another room, but I don't want to be far from him in case he does need me. "What are you doing?" he asks as I lay the cover on the chair.

Without looking at him, I answer, "I'm going to sleep here."

Out of the corner of my eye, I see him sit up. "You can't sleep in the chair. You won't be comfortable. Come to bed."

I look at him in our big king-size bed. It's so tempting to just lie down next to him. It's what I want to do, but I don't know if I should let myself. "I don't think it's a good idea," I tell him.

He holds both hands up. "Come on, Emery. I won't get any rest knowing that you're sleeping in that uncomfortable chair."

I know he's right. He will worry about me and most likely, I won't get any sleep either. I take a deep breath, walk back around to the other side of the bed, and crawl into my space, making sure to keep on my side of the bed. He lies down on his side, facing me, and I lie on my back and stare at the ceiling.

Uncomfortable with his gaze, I reach over and turn off the lamp and then assume the same position. He's quiet for so long, I almost wonder if he's asleep. But when I look over, he's still watching me in the darkness. I roll to my side and look at him worriedly. "What's going on with you, Nash? I hate to bring it up, but I have to. The doctor is obviously worried with all of the injuries you've had within the last year. What's going on?"

He lets out a deep breath. "I don't have a death wish. I know that's what he thought, but I don't. I've been careless. My focus hasn't been there. And in my position, in the job that I do, that's not a good thing."

I search his face, looking for all of the answers. I know what he's saying is that the divorce, us separating, is what caused this. "You agreed to the divorce. I thought you wanted it." His hand comes up and slides across the bed and stops right before it gets to me. He clenches the bedsheets and holds it there. It's like he wants to hold on to me but is not going to push it.

"You were so sad, Emery. You told me that you were not happy with me, and that gutted me because more than anything in this world, I want you to be happy. You deserve more than me. I know that. And that's why I let you go. And even though I know you deserve the moon, the stars, everything, I also know that there's no one on this earth that could love you like I do." My mind starts to go a hundred miles a minute. *Could it be as simple as that? He gave me a divorce because I asked him to, because I was unhappy?*

I reach over and lay my hand on top of his on the bed. He turns it over and clasps our hands together. "You can't keep doing this, Nash. You're going to get yourself killed."

He yawns and then mutters, "I know that. I'm going to make some changes."

As soon as the word *changes* comes out of his mouth, it's like I freeze up. I don't know how many times I've heard him say that before. I've begged and pleaded with him in the past. It's like I always wanted more of him than he was willing to give. I don't know how much I can trust in him saying that he's going to make a change. "Go ahead and sleep, Nash. I'll wake you up and check on you in an hour. I have my alarm set."

His hand tightens around mine. His voice is soft and almost slurring with tiredness. "I know that you don't believe me right now, Emery. But I'm going to prove it to you."

His words trail off into the darkness without a response from me. All I can do is hope that this time maybe it can be different.

Chapter 11

Nash

I wake up at some point in the middle of the night, and Emery is sprawled on top of me. I hold perfectly still, not wanting to move and chance her moving away from me. I lie here for I don't know how long trying to hold my breath but still trying to take it all in. It's like when we were married. Her curvy body against mine is like home to me.

I need to rest and let my body heal, but I don't want to waste time sleeping. Every second that I can, I want to spend it committing to memory this feeling right here. Emery groans in her sleep and lifts her leg over my body. I suck in a breath as her leg nudges against my hard cock. I hold in my groan as she fits her leg between my thighs. Her lower body shimmies back and forth, pressing itself into my leg.

I should be a gentleman and hold still, but I've never claimed to be one. I lift my leg a little higher and press it to her heated core. She whimpers in her sleep.

I would lie here all night letting her hump my leg, but I know she's not going to be happy with me if I do. Her head is on my chest, and I brush her hair away from her face and kiss her forehead. She moans my name.

It takes everything I have not to push her to her back and plunge deep inside of her. *You need to take this slowly, Nash. Don't fuck it up.* I tell myself that over and over. But her sleeping body is telling me what she needs. She needs to come.

I kiss her forehead again. "Emery, baby," I whisper.

She jolts awake, but I don't let her go far. I palm her ass, holding her to my leg. She lifts herself up an inch or two to look up at me. "Oh my God, I'm so sorry, Nash."

She tries again to roll away from me, but I don't let her. "You don't owe me an apology." She looks at me determinedly. "Let me go, Nash."

I release her, and she rolls over onto her back and throws her arm over her face. She tries to explain herself. "It's been a long time, but that doesn't mean I should take advantage of you when you're sick and hurt."

I roll toward her and lift her arm off of her face so I can see her eyes. "Honey, there would be no taking advantage of me."

She's looking at me, and the connection between us is like an electric wire zapping as the current goes through it.

I don't ask because I don't want her to tell me no. Instead, I lean down and press my lips to hers. She tries to hold back, lips pressed together, trying to put her guard up. But I'm not going to let her. I pull back and whisper against her lips, "Let me in."

I press my lips to hers again. She opens for me, and I plunge my tongue into her sweet depths. I kiss her for all I'm worth, wanting to show her exactly how much I love her, how much I've missed her, and how much I've needed her.

My hand goes down her shoulder onto her breasts, squeezing her, kneading her there. And then I trail my fingers down her belly. Her gown is high on her hips, and I go to her panty-covered pussy and touch the wet material at her most secret spot. She groans and pulls away.

Her hands go to each side of my neck, holding

me there in place. "I can't, Nash. I'm not ready for this, not yet."

I let my forehead fall to hers. I'm breathless as I answer her. "Let me make you come. Just let me make you feel good. That's all I want."

My hand is still between her legs, and when I feel her hips jerk, I take that as an answer. I pull her panties to the side and bare her pussy to me. I stroke through her swollen, wet lips and plunge knuckle deep into her channel, coating my finger with her wetness. I draw my finger up to her swollen clit, stroking it back and forth. She's ready. She's more than ready. She may not want to admit it, but she needs this.

I bring her close to the edge and then ease off. She moans and whimpers, and I do the same thing again, this time taking her completely over the edge. Her body is bucking against my hand, and I swallow her moan by fitting my mouth over hers.

Her orgasm races through her body, but I'm relentless in taking her to the edge over and over until she's completely spent. I release her, bringing my hand up to my mouth. She may not be ready for more, but I can't go another second without the taste of her on my lips. I've missed it. I suck her cream off my fingers, and my already hard cock gets even harder. I groan as I roll to my stomach and try to take deep breaths. The pain is relentless. It hurts like a son of a bitch, but it's worth it. Fuck it's worth it.

She puts her hand on my back, and I flinch. "Give me a second, baby."

"Nash, I can..."

But I shake my head and stop her. "No, we can wait until you're ready. I'll be good."

I keep taking deep breaths, letting my body calm down. When I'm able to get control, I roll onto my back and pull her body against me. One step at a time. I don't care how slowly I have to take it, Emery is worth it.

Chapter 12

Emery

"What are you doing here? I told you that we had it handled," Tara says as soon as I walk in the front doors of the Sugar Glaze Bakery.

It's been four days since Nash was shot, and I left him at home making him promise that he would stay on the couch until I got back. But I had to get out of there.

Slowly I've been letting my guard down, and how could I not, when Nash is saying and doing everything right? He hasn't touched me again like he did that first night, but he still kisses me and holds my hand every chance he gets. It's slowly driving me mad, and more and more I want to say hell with protecting my heart and go for it.

I shrug my shoulders at Tara. "I just wanted to come in and check on things."

She puts her hand on her hip, obviously seeing right through me. "No, you just wanted to get away from your hot husband."

I roll my eyes. "First of all, he's not my husband."

She barks out a laugh. "Have you told him that? Because he sure follows you around with those big puppy dog eyes like he wants to be."

I close my eyes and try to clear my head. "I just needed a break."

That seems to alarm her. "Is everything okay? I thought Nash was all right."

I walk behind the counter. "Yes, everything is all right, and Nash is going to be okay. I just don't know. All these old feelings..."

Tara has always been one to say it exactly as it is. "They're not old feelings, Emery. You've felt them this whole time. It may have taken him a while to get his shit together, but I really think he's trying. He's been stalking your ass for the last year. You should at least give him a chance."

I shake my head. "It's not that. He's getting better. His arm is good. His vision and head is good. He's going to be leaving soon."

Tara doesn't even hesitate in her response. "Did he tell you that?"

I shake my head. "I mean, no, he didn't say that, but of course that's what's going to happen. As soon as he's healed, he's going to go back on his missions and probably get hurt again." I throw my hands up in the air. "I can't do this."

Tara comes to me and grabs on to my hand and holds it tightly. "Tell him that. He needs to hear you say that."

I look her in the eye. "And what? He won't go and then resent me for it? No, thanks. I'll just keep my guard up and bide my time until he leaves again and then pick up the pieces of my broken heart... AGAIN."

Tara pulls me in and hugs me. "I think he's going to surprise you this time."

I don't even want to let myself hope. I pull back and look at the bakery. Everything is clean, and it doesn't even look like they've missed me. Changing the subject, I ask her, "So what have I missed here? How are you and Mark doing?"

Mark is her boyfriend, and I hate to say it, but he's not the best. I'm just trying to be supportive.

Tara rolls her eyes. "I broke up with Mark."

When I start to tell her I'm sorry, she stops me and holds her hand up. "No, it's fine. It was for the best."

It's my turn to pull her in for a hug. "Are you okay?"

She nods. "Yeah, I'm fine."

In the next instant, there's the sound of motorcycles, and they all seem to stop outside the bakery. "What in the world?"

Becca comes from the back of the bakery and is surprised when she sees me standing there. "Oh hey, Emery." And then she looks at Tara. "Really, you couldn't find some boring boy that likes to hang out at the bakery? Instead, you find some biker from a GANG that can't seem to get enough of your strawberry pie."

I look between Becca and Tara. "What is she talking about?"

Becca throws me an apron. "Oh, just wait and see. It's good you're here. We can use you for the next 20-30 minutes. They've been wiping us out."

I barely get the apron tied before around fifteen bikers come in the front door. I know I'm staring, but this is definitely something different for Whiskey Run.

The first man walks straight toward Tara. "How's it going, Mama?"

I look at Becca and mouth *Mama?* to her with my mouth hanging open.

Becca nods and then mouths back, *Watch*.

Tara hands a slice of strawberry pie to the man and then walks away. The dark-haired man watches her, obviously liking what he sees. "That's okay, Mama. You're going to give in eventually 'cause me and you are meant to be."

Tara rolls her eyes. "In your dreams, biker boy."

He laughs good-naturedly. "You're right about that."

We spend the next half hour dishing out desserts to the bikers and then they get some to go. I can't help but watch the way the one they call Jason keeps watching Tara. It's obvious he's hooked, and she's trying to act as if she's not interested at all, but I know her... she's definitely into him.

When they leave and Jason promises to see Tara tomorrow, I whirl around. "What in the world was that?"

Becca laughs. "That is the new biker gang in town."

"Club. They're not a gang. They're a club," Tara corrects her.

Becca just laughs some more. "Yeah, okay, that's the new biker club, and Tara here seems to have caught the eye of one of them. They've came in every day, order everything we have, and they even clean up after themselves. We've had to bake extra and even keep some stuff stored in the back just to make it through the evenings."

I look at Tara. "Jason seems nice. He definitely doesn't like any of his friends looking at you."

She blushes. "I'm not interested."

I don't believe her for a minute. We spend the next half hour with Tara filling me in on special orders and events. I could spend the rest of the afternoon here catching up on paperwork, but I'm anxious to get back to Nash.

I walk out the door, and I tell Tara to call me if she needs anything. I stop at the store and then go back home, and I'm surprised when I get there that Nash has fixed dinner. The table is set with lit candles and a chilled bottle of wine. I set down the small bag of groceries with just the staples of bread and milk.

"You fixed dinner," I said, surprised.

He grabs the bag and unloads the groceries. "Yeah, but don't get too excited. It's only spaghetti."

I look at him curiously. "I love spaghetti, especially your spaghetti."

He smiles at that. "I know you do."

I can feel the butterflies in my stomach as he leads me over to the table. I drink a glass of wine, and I can feel myself loosening up around him. We talk about any and everything. Well, everything except for past hurts. It seems as if we both try to avoid anything that will bring that up.

I have to keep reminding myself that Nash and I are divorced, that this probably won't go anywhere, but the more we sit here and laugh, the harder that is to do. When we finish eating, he all but pushes me out of the kitchen and tells me to relax in the living room, he's going to clean up.

"You're the one that's hurt. Let me clean up."

He shakes his head, stopping me from going into the kitchen. "I feel great. No headaches, vision is good. I'm good."

I tilt my head and know he's telling the truth but also knowing it's not right for him to cook and have to clean up. "Nash, I'm serious."

He still doesn't let me in. "I got this. Let me do this. I'll be in in a minute."

I go and sit down, and I feel a little weird sitting on the couch as he cleans up. I can hear the dishwasher going, and he joins me a second later, two glasses of wine in his hands. He brings one to me and then sits next to me on the couch.

"Talk to me," he says.

I shrug and take a sip of the wine before setting it on the coaster on the table. "What do you want to talk about?"

He reaches for my hand and laces our fingers together. "For starters why you ran out of here this afternoon."

I tense up, already not liking where this conversation is heading. "I just needed to check on the bakery."

He smiles at me. "I know you, Emery. There was more to it than that."

And I realize I just need to put it all out in the open, lay it all out for him. "I needed to put some distance between us. It would be so easy to get used to this, to having you around like this. I needed to get my head back on right."

He sighs, "I regret all of the missions that I left you to go on. If I could go back and change the way I did things, I would. I just need to know that it's not too late to change things and to make things right."

I shake my head. "I don't know, Nash. I can't ask you... I just don't know." All I can think about is just how unbearable it was without him. Would I rather have him half the time than not at all? I'm second-guessing everything now, and it seems like everything is jumbling around in my head.

"Talk to me," he says.

I open my mouth, but then close it.

He leans toward me, and his hand goes to my shoulder and squeezes me there. "What do you want, Emery? If you could have anything, what would that be?"

Without even thinking about it, I blurt out the first thing that comes into my head. "A baby."

Chapter 13

Nash

She looks at me, her eyes rounded, and blinks. "I want a baby. I want your baby."

We stare at one another until there's no holding back. I set the wine glass on the coffee table and lean toward her. Our lips mesh together like an uncontrollable force. I pull her toward me until our bodies are flush against each other. In the past, hearing the word *baby* would've made me run, would've scared me to death. But now just the thought of Emery pregnant, rounded with our child makes my cock hard and my heart race in my chest.

We're grabbing at each other's clothes, pulling them off. It's not graceful or calm. We don't stop until we're both naked before each other, like we're in a rush, desperate to have one another.

And I know that we need to slow it down. "Are you sure about this, Emery? I don't want to rush you. I can wait."

She kisses my neck. "I'm sure."

Her hot breath hits against my skin as she moves down my chest. When her lips wrap around my nipple and she suckles me there, I groan, wrapping my hand around her hair, holding her to me. "Fuck yeah," I say.

Her hand trails down my body, and she wraps her hand around my hard length. She strokes me, and already I can feel the pre-cum at the tip of my cock. I'm needy, and I'm not going to be able to hold back for long. She pushes me backwards onto the couch. She stands over me, and my gaze travels from her head, down her body, taking in her large breasts, soft belly, and wide hips. My mouth is watering, wanting her. I reach up, grasping on to her hips, digging my fingers into her skin. She moans, lifting one leg and putting it on the couch next to my thigh before lifting her other until she straddles me. She moves her hips back and forth, coating my dick with her arousal.

My head falls back onto the couch. So close. I'm so close.

"That feels good, Nash," she says.

I lift my head and look at her through hooded eyes. "I need to be inside you, Emery. Please don't make me wait."

She smiles, knowing that she has all the power here. I am weak when it comes to her. She could ask me for anything right now, and I would give it to her. She raises up on her knees and reaches between us, gripping my hardness in the palm of her hand. She strokes me once, twice, and then positions me at her swollen entrance. She sinks down on me slowly, and I hold my breath. I don't let it out until she's fully seated and I'm balls deep inside of her. The need to thrust overcomes me, and I lift my hips, grabbing on to her, holding her as I pummel inside of her. She moves back and forth. We find a rhythm that is raw and satisfying. So close. I'm so close. I need her to come with me.

I reach between us and put my thumb on her clit, moving it back and forth quickly. She moans and groans over me, but she doesn't stop. Up and down she moves. "Yes, baby. Take me, take all of me."

She's fighting it. She's holding on to her orgasm, but I need her to let go. "Let me in, Emery. Let me in, baby. Let me fill you with my seed. Let me make you pregnant."

That's all it takes for an earth-shattering orgasm

to shoot through her body, and almost instantly, it does the same to me. I shoot rope after rope of cum deep within her womb. My body is filled with tiny vibrations, and I feel it from my feet through my body, to the ends of my fingertips.

I lie here trying to calm the rapid beat of my heart. Emery sprawls on my chest, gasping for breath.

I'm so fucking tired, and I don't want to move, but I also know that I need Emery in our bed. I put my arm arms around her and squeeze her. "Hold on to me, honey."

She wraps her arms around my neck, and I stand up. "No, Nash. I'm too heavy."

I swat her on the ass. "Don't say that."

She nuzzles against my chest, and I carry her out of the living room, up the stairs into our bedroom. As soon as I lay her down, I go to the bathroom and get stuff to clean us up. And as soon as that is finished, I lie down next to her and wrap my arms and legs around her, hoping and praying that she doesn't regret this.

Chapter 14

Emery

I'm wrapped in Nash's arms, and I can't imagine another place I'd rather be. But already, I'm starting to have second thoughts. I try to make light of the situation. "Obviously, pain pills and alcohol don't mix well," I say to him.

He grunts before he kisses the top of my head. "I haven't taken any of the pain pills. And I only had half a glass of wine."

I pull away from his arms a little and get up on my elbows to look at him. "We probably should have talked about all of this first."

He doesn't let me go far. He still has his hand on my back and his legs over mine. "Talked about what?"

"Nash, I'm not on the pill anymore. When we got a divorce, I didn't think I needed it."

He shrugs as if it's not a big deal. "That's good, right? I mean, you wanted a baby." He's watching me closely, and I try not to let the emotion show on my face. He's right, I do want a baby. But what about him? I look at my hands, twiddling with my fingers. "I'm just saying that if I do get pregnant, it doesn't have to change anything. I can take care of him or her on my own. I don't want..." But he doesn't let me finish.

He interrupts me, and his whole body gets tense next to mine. "You don't want me in the picture?"

I shake my head. "That's not what I meant."

His voice raises. "Well, what did you mean? It sounds to me like you want a kid, but it doesn't matter if I'm around or not."

I blow out a breath in frustration. "You know that's not true. I've always wanted you, Nash, but you are unreachable."

He lifts up on his elbow and puts his head in his palm, staring at me. "You're right. We should have talked first."

I shake my head. "I wasn't trying to trap you. I'm sorry, Nash. This doesn't have to change anything."

For just a second, he looks mad. It's as if I can visibly see him count to 10 as he watches me. I know that every emotion is showing on my face: insecurity, fear, hope. All of it is right there for him to see. I don't even try to hide it. He takes a deep breath, reaches for my hand, and holds on to it. He mutters the words that bring even more hope to me. "What if I want it to change?"

My eyes widen. "What do you mean?"

He pulls me toward him until our bodies are flush once again against each other. "What if I want it to change everything?"

Damn, I want to believe him. I so much want to believe that everything can be different this time around. But I know I won't survive it if it's not the case. I blurt it all out. "I can't do that again, Nash. Do you have any idea what it's like when you leave? I'm scared the whole time that something is going to happen to you. Hell, look at this last year, all those things. I can't do it."

He puts his hand on my cheek and looks at me without blinking. "I'm not traveling anymore, Emery. At least not like that. I'm not going on missions. We promoted Colt, and we're hiring more people. Everything I do will be from Whiskey Run."

"But..." I start, and he holds his hand up to stop me.

"Listen to me. I've already talked to Walker.

Before any of this happened, I talked to him and put everything in motion. I'm done with all of the traveling. The only thing that I want is to be close to you and to our family. If we have our own kids, if we adopt, whatever it is that you want, that's what I want. And I know I'm gonna to fuck up along the way, but I'm going to count on you to tell me and give me a chance to make it right."

I look down at the bed because it hurts to look at him. I don't want him to resent me. "Nash, you're going to miss it."

He puts his finger on the bottom of my chin and lifts my face to where I look at him.

"I miss you, Emery. I can go forever without doing another mission, but I can't go another day without you. I need you. I've loved you this whole time, and I'll never stop. From this point on, I'm going to be the man that you need. The man that you want. That's all that matters to me."

I start to cry because how could I not? It's like he's giving me everything I want, granting me my wish. I dive on top of him, kissing him, and he laughs as he holds on to me. I'm not a fool. I know there are going to be issues that come up, but with Nash by my side, we can work through it.

"I love you so much, Nash."

He kisses me until I'm breathless and pulls back, resting his forehead against mine. "I love you too, baby."

Epilogue

Nash

Five Years Later

"Hunter Nash Jr! You better get down from there before your mama comes out here and spanks us both."

I watch as my five-year-old son climbs down from the big playset. He comes toward me with a big smile on his face, and I shake my head. "Hunter, you know you are supposed to hang from the monkey bars, not walk across the top of them."

Right then Emery comes out of the house with our daughter Avery on her hip. She looks between

Hunter and me, shaking her head. "Like father, like son."

I don't think she's meaning it as a compliment, but I smile anyway. Six years ago, if anyone had told me that I'd be settled down, no more traveling on missions, with two kids AND happy, I wouldn't have believed them. I'm not going to lie; when we got the call about Hunter, I was scared to death. I hadn't known it, but Emery had applied at some adoption agencies. When she got the call that not only she was accepted but they had a baby that needed emergency placement, we immediately said yes.

In the span of two weeks, Emery and I got remarried, decorated a nursery, our friends threw us a baby shower, and we became parents. It was definitely a whirlwind.

Emery worried about me. She kept waiting for me to freak out, take off on a mission or something else crazy, but I never did. And when we went to the hospital and picked up Hunter Jr., my whole life changed. I no longer feared that I would let my son down. I knew from the first moment I looked into his eyes that I would do anything and everything to love and protect him until the day I die.

Emery stops next to me, and Avery holds her hands out. "Dada!"

I can't resist her. I take her from Emery, and Emery rolls her eyes. "I don't get it. I carried her for nine months and gained all the weight. I'm the one that went through twelve hours of labor. You would think her first word would be Momma!"

I kiss Avery's head and then move her to my hip so I can put my arm around Emery. She nuzzles against me, and I stare down at her, still not believing that she's mine. "Let's not talk about the delivery."

She shakes her head and looks up at me with sympathy. "Nash, you have to get over that. I'm fine, and Avery was fine."

I kiss Avery's head and set her down in the grass. "Hunter, watch your sis for a minute."

He walks over and sits down next to Avery and rolls a ball to her. "You got it, Dad."

I grab on to Emery's hand and walk up on the porch where we can still keep an eye on the kids but also get some privacy. I put my arms around her waist and hold on to her, breathing her in.

She usually melts into my embrace, but this time she's holding herself rigid. "What is it, Nash? What's wrong?"

My voice is gruff when I answer her. "You're okay now, Emery. But those twelve hours you were in labor were the longest of my life."

She just smirks and laughs like I made some kind of joke, and I'm not having it. I rest my chin on the top of her head and try not to get lost in the memories. "I'm not joking. I have lain in a wet swamp for ten hours, anticipating the perfect time to move to safety. I've had to sit completely still for fourteen hours, no sleep and make sure that I don't move a muscle as we set in enemy territory surrounded by fifty men and pray to God that we were not found before help arrived. I've trekked across the mountains of Afghanistan on high alert as we helped ten women that had been trafficked across the border. I've been tortured, shot, burned... and with all of that, watching you in pain, seeing what you were going through and I couldn't do anything to help was the absolute worst thing I've ever experienced in my life."

Emery reaches up and puts her hands on each side of my face, forcing me to look at her. "Nash... I didn't know... I had no idea."

I shake my head, visibly shaken from the memories. "I couldn't stand seeing you like that."

She shakes her head. "No, I mean, I knew what you did, but I had no idea everything you DID. Oh Nash... that's horrible, I couldn't imagine."

I turn my head, holding her hand and kissing her palm. "That part of my life is over, Emery."

She tilts her head. "Do you regret quitting?"

I shrug. "Regret it... never. This... you... the kids... that makes me happy. Do I feel guilty sometimes? I do... I know I shouldn't, but it's hard sometimes being here and knowing my brothers are fighting and I'm not there to help...even though I know what I'm doing from the compound is important too... it's just different."

Emery is quiet, no doubt reflecting on everything she just learned. I've kept it to myself for so long. This probably wasn't the best way to tell her.

She puts her cheek against my chest. I look at Hunter and Avery, and they're still playing with the ball. "Okay, what's wrong?"

I know my wife, and there's something on her mind. I thought I'd let her come to me with it, but she obviously needs some pushing.

"I have something to tell you."

I laugh at the rigid tone in her voice. She's actually nervous about this, and there's no reason for her to be. She can tell me anything. "You can tell me anything... except that you're pregnant," I joke.

Her whole body freezes against mine, and my

mouth goes dry. Oh hell, no. I pull back and search her face. "Are you pregnant?"

She bites on to her lower lip and nods her head slowly.

Emotions from all ranges of the spectrum hit me. I'm happy, excited, scared, worried. It's all right there.

She looks at me nervously. "Please, don't be mad or upset."

I know I need to man up here. The thought of her going through it all again is smothering to me, but I need to be strong for her. I lean down and kiss her. She moans, and I deepen the kiss, putting all my love, every emotion, into it. When I pull back, breathless, I lean my forehead against hers. "I'm not mad or upset. I'm happy. You... our family, makes me happy. I'll just have a talk with the doctor and tell him we need to speed things up this time."

She laughs, and I take in the way she's absolutely glowing. I should have known something was up. She pats me on the chest. "I don't think it works that way, Nash."

I shrug my shoulders. "It will. I don't want to see you in pain like that again."

She looks at me with a crease in her forehead. "I don't even remember it."

I wait for her to laugh, but she doesn't. My mouth falls open. "You don't remember it?"

This time she does laugh and shakes her head. "No, I don't remember the pain at all. You know what I remember about that day? I remember seeing you and Hunter holding our daughter for the first time. I remember you with a tear on your cheek because you felt so much love and emotion that you couldn't hold it in. I remember you holding me, Hunter, and Avery all together on that little hospital bed and never feeling more loved than I did in that moment. That's what I remember, Nash."

I'm looking at her with such awe. I still don't know what I did to deserve her, but I'm a lucky man. "Fuck, I love you, baby."

For the first time, she doesn't get on to me for cursing in front of the kids. She puts her arms around my waist. "I love you too, Nash."

I kiss her one more time. "Okay, so are we telling them they're going to have a little brother or sister?"

She looks at me excitedly. "Yes, let's do it."

And together, hand in hand, we join our kids, and I'm once again in awe that this is my life. Emery saved me by giving me a second chance, and I'll never take that for granted.

Get Tara and Jason's story in Bad Boy Love

Want more of Nash and the Ghost Team heroes? Get it in the Whiskey Run: Heroes series.

Whiskey Run Series

Want more of Whiskey Run?

Whiskey Run

Faithful - He's the hot, say-it-like-it-is cowboy, and he won't stop until he gets the woman he wants.

Captivated - She's a beautiful woman on the run... and I'm going to be the one to keep her.

Obsessed - She's loved him since high school and now he's back.

Seduced - He's a football player that falls in love with the small town girl.

Devoted - She's a plus size model and he's a small town mechanic.

Whiskey Run: Savage Ink

Virile - He won't let her go until he puts his mark on her.

Torrid - He'll do anything to give her what she wants.

Rigid - If you love reading about emotionally wounded men and the women that help them overcome their past, then you'll love Dawson and Emily's story.

Whiskey Run: Cowboys Love Curves

Obsessed Cowboy - She's the preacher's daughter and she's

off limits.

Whiskey Run: Heroes

Ransom - He's on a mission he can't lose.

Redeem - He's in love with his sister's best friend.

Submit - She's his fake wife but he wants to make it real.

Forbid - They have a secret romance but he's about to stake his claim.

Whiskey Run: Sugar

One Night Love - Her one night stand wants more.

Rebound Love - She's falling for the rebound guy.

Second Chance Love - He is not a man to ignore… especially when he asks for a second chance.

Bad Boy Love - He's a bad boy that wants her good.

Free Books

Want FREE BOOKS?
Go to www.authorhopeford.com/freebies

JOIN ME!

JOIN MY NEWSLETTER & READERS GROUP

www.AuthorHopeFord.com/Subscribe

JOIN MY READERS GROUP ON FACEBOOK

www.FB.com/groups/hopeford

Find Hope Ford at www.authorhopeford.com

About the Author

USA Today Bestselling Author Hope Ford writes short, steamy, sweet romances. She loves tattooed, alpha men, instant love stories, and ALWAYS happily ever afters. She has over 100 books and they are all available on Amazon.

To find me on Pinterest, Instagram, Facebook, Goodreads, and more:

www.AuthorHopeFord.com/follow-me

Manufactured by Amazon.ca
Bolton, ON